Dedication

*To the people of Georgetown, South Carolina who have
welcomed us with friendly smiles, warm hearts,
and loving arms...*

*thank you all for making us feel so welcome in
our new home!*

~ Christine and Tom Doran

"Help protect our waterways!"

Flash and Fancy

An Otter Adventure
on the Waccamaw River

Written by
Tom Doran and Christine Thomas Doran

Illustrated by Nancy Van Buren

Flash and Fancy
An Otter Adventure on the Waccamaw River
Copyright © 2015
Tom Doran and Christine Thomas Doran

Comments
clocktowerbookspublishing@gmail.com

Illustrations by
Nancy Van Buren

ISBN: 978-1-941069-34-9

Clock Tower Books Publishing
Georgetown, SC 29440

clocktowerbookspublishing@gmail.com
www.clocktowerbooksgeorgetown.com

Acknowledgements

Many wonderful people and environmental programs have influenced us in our endeavor to make Flash and Fancy come to life.

We would like to especially thank:

Brookgreen Gardens for their fantastic otter habitat display and learning lab. We spent a lot of time watching the playful behavior and habits of the otters, as well as listening to their unique language.

The Public Boat Tour of Winyah Bay at Hobcaw Barony Discovery Center, North Inlet-Winyah Bay National Estuarine Research Reserve, University of South Carolina, and the South Carolina Department of Natural Resources.

Waccamaw Riverkeeper Program of the Winyah Rivers Foundation whose mission is to protect and to conserve the Waccamaw River. This environmental program stresses the importance of being sensitive to our flora and fauna whose very existence depends on our river. If the Waccamaw River is unprotected, our wildlife will become endangered.

Georgetown River Sweep organized by Keep Georgetown Beautiful and sponsored by the Department of Natural Resources and the South Carolina Sea Grant Consortium.

South Carolina Department of Natural Resources Website which provided a fountain of information on river otters and the gorgeous coastal environment.

Michele Overton and Clock Tower Books Publishing who gave us the encouragement and the opportunity to make our dream of writing an informative yet delightful story about two otters become a reality.

Bob O'Brien from Prose Press who created a professional finished product.

Nancy Van Buren, who painted our words with her splendid lifelike illustrations.

It was a new summer's day on Sandy Island.
The stirrings of forest wetland creatures filled the warm,
misty morning air after a long night's slumber.
In the stillness of dawn, a deep chorus of bullfrogs was like
a sunrise symphony,"**Groarrrk, groarrk, groarrk!**"
They were interrupted occasionally by the high trills of
tree frogs, "**Trrrilll, trrrilll, trrrilll!**"

The whispery flutter of an egret's wings brushed near the river's surface. Its alabaster wings were a sharp contrast to the dark tea-colored water of the Waccamaw River. The spectacular river was the color of tea because of the tannic acid that is found in the cypress tree needles that have fallen into the water. Tea-colored water is also due to the decaying leaves of other trees and plants that have fallen into the water along the river's marshy edge. Off in the distance, the faint tapping of a red-headed woodpecker could be heard from inside the thick forest. Suddenly, a sleek, streamlined river otter peeked its sleepy face out from its holt, or den.

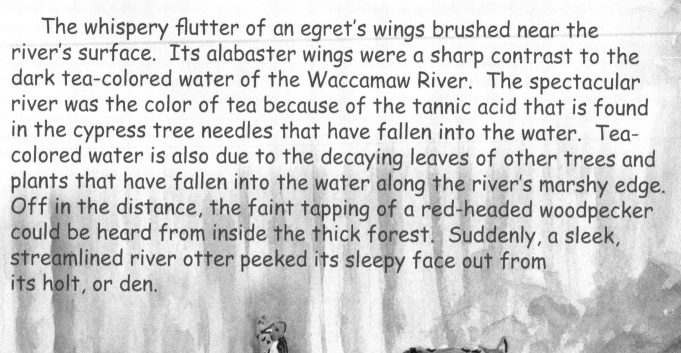

3

Ambling slowly through a Spanish moss draped forest of bald cypress, tupelo pine, and water oak, the young male otter arrived at the marshy edge of the Waccamaw River.

Once he entered the dark river, the otter joyously swam with little effort, and he did what otters do best: PLAY! "Ah! This is the life!" he burbled.

The playful creature was in a state of ecstasy! He used his webbed paws and short, powerful front and back legs to propel himself through the rippling, rushing water as easily as an Olympic swimmer. His long, tapered tail helped to steady him as he darted in and out of the churning water.

"WooHoo!" the otter chirped. He rolled and whirled over and over through the water, and he swam as fast as a flash of lightning! That was why all of his otter friends in the coastal river habitat called this speedy otter, **Flash.**

"Purr, purr, purr," gurgled the feisty otter. His dark brown, luscious fur gleamed in the glow of the morning light. Flash's small head, including his bright eyes, large triangular shaped nose, long thick whiskers, and tiny ears could be seen above the glimmering water as he gracefully glided.

"Woowhee! Woowhee! Woowhee!" Suddenly, the shrill whistle of another otter filled the peaceful morning air! This signal meant danger! As fast as the speed of light, Flash sped in the direction of the grassy, cattail lined water's edge. In the distance, he saw a young female otter entangled in a carelessly discarded casting net! Dangerous litter from humans seemed to be ruining his beautiful habitat more and more each day.

"Help me! Help me! My paw is stuck!" she frantically cried out in a voice full of pain.

Flash recognized her as an otter named **Fancy**. All her otter friends called her Fancy because around her neck was a silvery gray band of fur. Against her chocolate brown, luxurious coat, this band of fur looked like a twinkling necklace.

⊱⊰⊱

Fancy lifted her beautiful, soft, whiskered face to the sweet scented morning air. "Woowhee! Woowhee! Woowhee! Please help me!" the dainty otter desperately whistled.

As the dark water of the Waccamaw River swirled around her, terror shone in her luminous eyes! Her heart pounded fast and hard in her chest while she desperately clutched onto the slippery submerged branch of a fallen tree. Over and over again, the young otter tried to kick herself free of the net that was tightly tangled around her back paw, but she was still unable to break herself free no matter how hard she tried!

Fancy hoped an otter friend would hear her frantic cries and come to her rescue! She feared a predator, like a quick-moving bobcat or a hungry feral hog, might hear her distress signal cries instead!

Without warning, Fancy heard the churning of water. At first, fear gripped her heart, but then she recognized a handsome male otter named Flash! He was speeding in her direction like a torpedo!

"Chirrrp! Chirrrp! Chirrp! I will save you, Fancy!" he cried out. Flash had learned long ago that swimming well was not only for play, but it was also needed for survival. This superb swimmer rocketed confidently towards Fancy and the submerged casting net!

Using his small nimble paws, the strong young otter tried several times to untangle Fancy's back right paw. In the meantime, Fancy continued to try to pull her paw loose from the net, but this caused it to tighten even more!

"Owww! Owww!" she screamed out in pain.

"Please be still, Fancy! I will have you freed soon! I promise! Hold fast!" chattered Flash.

As the sleek otter dived beneath the surface towards the net, his nose and ears closed, which kept out the river water. This amazing swimmer could stay underwater for up to four minutes!

Flash resurfaced briefly, but then he immediately sensed another danger! His sensitive whiskers picked up the scent of a nearby animal from the woods. A young bobcat lurked in the shadows of a group of bald cypress trees near the river bank!

"Grrr! Grrr! Grrr!" growled the wild bobcat as it stealthily approached. He tried to camouflage himself among some of the long hanging Spanish moss that dangled from the trees.

The courageous young otter made one more careful but firm lunge at the casting net. Using his powerful wedge-shaped nose, sharp teeth, and delicate and dexterous paws, he released the trapped little otter.

"There! You are free now, Fancy! You don't have to be afraid anymore," chortled Flash.

"Oh, thank you, thank you, Flash!" squealed a very grateful Fancy. Her beautiful dark eyes sparkled at him in the warm morning sunlight. Her heart still pounded strongly in her chest, but this time it was not from fear, but from relief and excitement!

"Come on, Fancy! Let's go for a swim!" chattered the brave male otter. He was feeling very proud of himself for having rescued a young female otter in distress!

In a demure voice Fancy answered, "That sounds like a lot of fun, Flash." She looked up at him shyly and fluttered her long eyelashes.

Grasping Fancy's small front paw with his larger and stronger paw, Flash slowly guided Fancy through the strong currents. He knew her back paw must be sore, and he didn't want to hurt her further. Fancy felt relieved and thrilled to be rescued! Flash had saved her life!

Swimming to freedom, the refreshing river was their water park! Once in the deep water, Fancy's paw barely hurt at all!

"Catch me if you can!" Flash chuckled and chirped with pleasure as they played a delightful game of chase. Simultaneously, they swirled, twirled, and pirouetted like dancers in a water ballet.

"Chachee! Chachee! Chachee! Wheee! Whee!" they chattered as they slid down a roller coaster of rocks worn smooth as silk by the cascading water. At the bottom, they splashed down to a frenzied bout of water tag. Finally, exhausted from play, Flash and Fancy swam closely side by side until they reached the opposite bank of the Waccamaw River.

The otters came upon a large grassy area surrounded by cattails. There they collapsed and basked in the bright warm sunshine. In the stillness of the early afternoon, the buzzing of lacy winged dragonflies hovered over the water like tiny helicopters. "Zzzz...Zzzz...Zzzz." Soon the gentle sound lulled them to sleep.

Awhile later, refreshed from their nap, Fancy purred softly, "Come on Flash! I want you to meet my family!" They bounded along the edge of the river to the holt that Fancy shared with her family of otters. It was a warm, snug, and cozy little den made of soft grass, moss, bark, leaves and fur.

It was getting later in the day, and the tide had fallen. Flash decided to surprise Fancy and her family. He wanted them to know how much he cared about their oldest otter daughter. The Waccamaw River provides a vast assortment of aquatic food that otters love to eat. Flash knew just what to do!

He rubbed his little paws together and thought, "Boy, oh boy! Are we going to have a feast!"

The excited otter returned to the Waccamaw River. There he spied, reached out, and gathered several luscious exposed clams and juicy crayfish that had come in with the tide. He laid them carefully along the shore of Sandy Island among the tall, flowing marsh grasses close to Fancy's holt.

Next, Flash approached the swiftly flowing water of the river. He took a deep breath, and then down, down, down he dived to depths nearing twenty feet, although otters can dive as deep as sixty feet! This expert swimmer could swim six to seven miles per hour!

Suddenly, a large school of slow moving pumpkinseed sunfish, mixed with bluegill, striped bass, and silver perch swam in his direction. Flash used his sensitive whiskers and keen sense of touch to expertly and quickly catch several fish. His cream colored belly fur helped to camouflage him as he approached his prey. With each catch, the amazing river otter placed the succulent fish upon the grassy river bank.

Then, one by one, Flash took the tasty prizes to his new friends' holt. There, the river otters devoured their freshwater feast that was fit for a king! "Chirp... chirp... chirp," they warbled in delight.

During their chatty dinner party, Flash and Fancy excitedly talked to Fancy's family about their thrilling day! Everyone talked at once and asked so many questions about the daring rescue. They all agreed that Flash was a hero! "Hip hip hooray! Hip hip hooray for Flash!" the otters chortled wildly!

When no one was listening, Flash and Fancy whispered to each other and promised to stay best friends forever. This was a very special promise because otters do not usually stay together. Flash was such an honorable otter. "I will always be near you, and I will always try to protect you from any dangers out there," he bravely promised Fancy.

At last, it was time to leave, and an extremely tired Flash slowly lumbered out of Fancy's cozy holt. He found his way back through the thick forest of trees until he came upon his own comfortable and secure home in a fallen tree log.

As he curled up into his soft nest, the young otter dreamed of the amazing otter adventure on the mighty Waccamaw River. "Purrr, purrr, purrr," he murmured in his contented sleep.

Like a soft velvet blanket, the stillness of twilight settled over
the diverse habitats of the coastal river ecosystem.
"Hoot! Hoot!" A solitary owl's cry pierced the darkness.

Flickering lightning bugs sparkled like miniature
lanterns in the warm, summer evening air.
For Flash and Fancy, another exciting day
had ended on Sandy Island.

The End

CPSIA information can be obtained
at www.ICGtesting.com
Printed in the USA
BVHW022324260120
570503BV00004B/19